LITTLE ANT ON THE GO

written and illustrated by

Ilene Dudek

Dedicated to my boys, Matthew and Alex, who are always on the go –
keep chasing that adventure!

Little Ant on the Go

Printed in the United States of America by CreateSpace, an Amazon company.

ISBN 978-0-692-89507-8

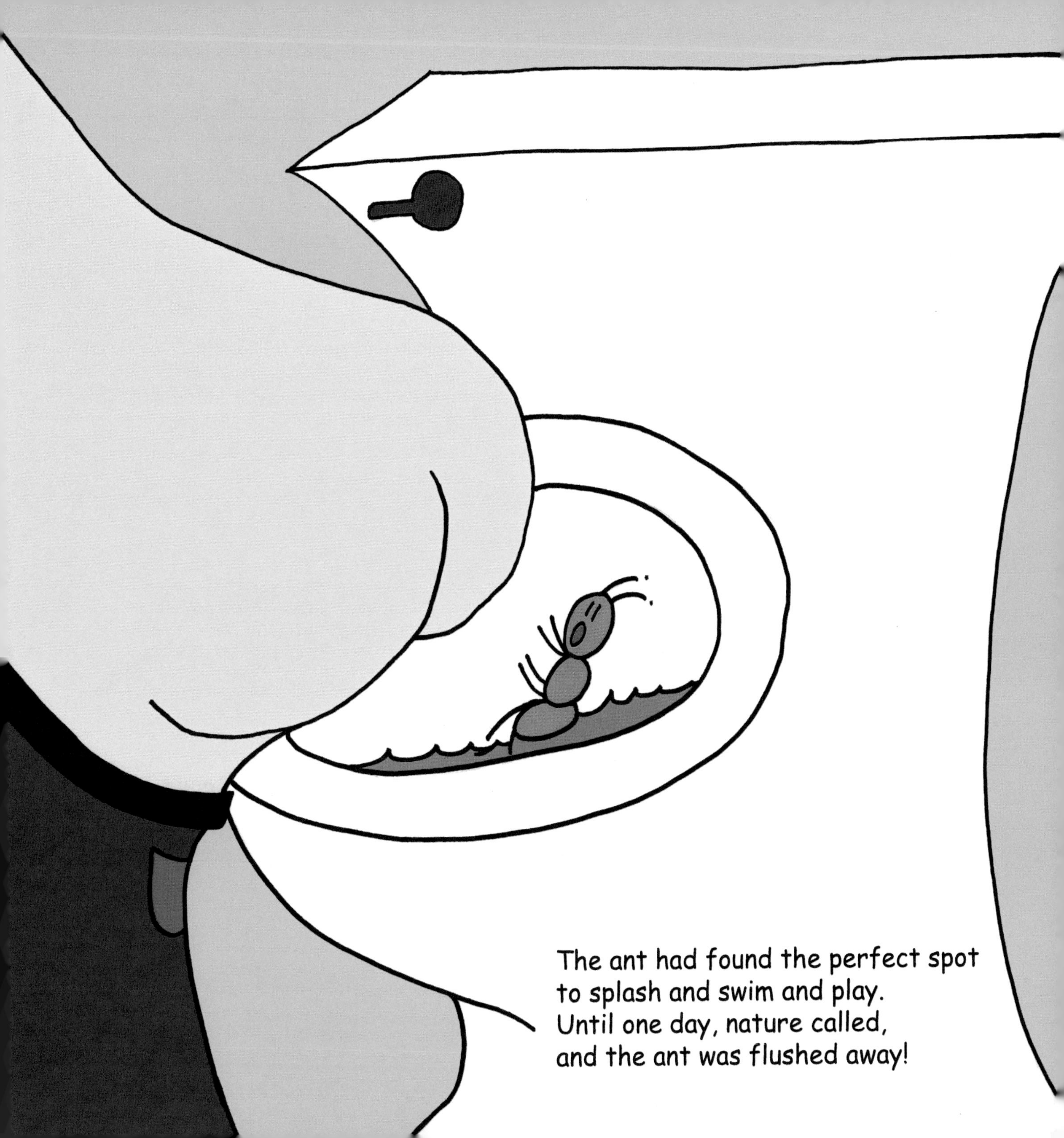
The ant had found the perfect spot
to splash and swim and play.
Until one day, nature called,
and the ant was flushed away!

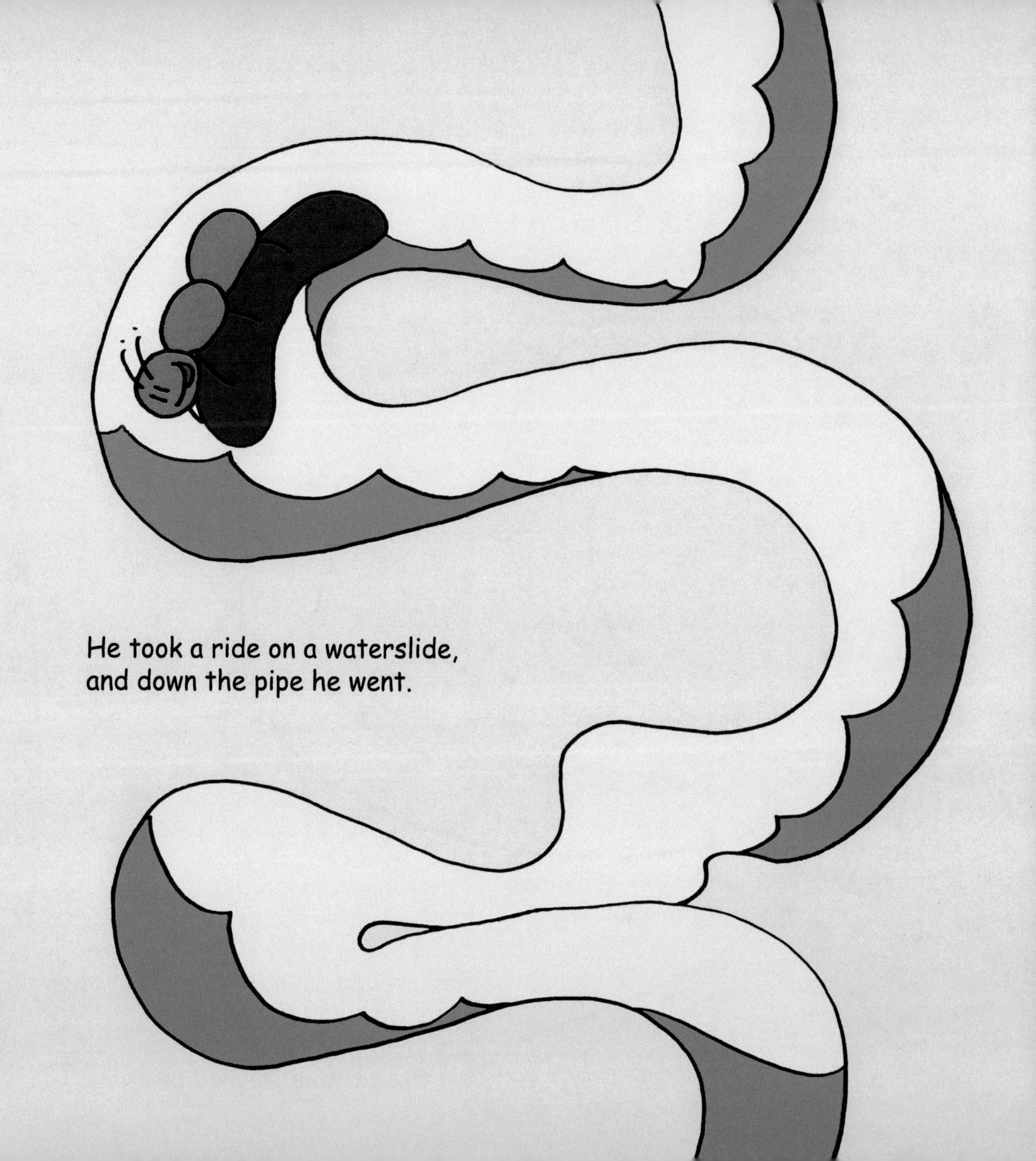
He took a ride on a waterslide,
and down the pipe he went.

Whee! Into the sea.
And whoa! There he goes,
right into the mouth of a whale.

It didn't take long for the whale to shout,
"Take a ride on my waterspout!"

And up...and up...and up he went!

And down he fell into a fisherman's boat.
BAIT

He was hooked like a worm and thrown to the fishes,
and one of them thought he was truly delicious!

But this was his chance to get away,
for that fish would be the catch of the day.
BAIT

Once ashore, he heard the cries
of hungry seagulls flying by.
And bopped a big one in the nose
for nibbling on his tiny toes.

Hot sand! Hot feet!
Cool shells were a nice treat
to get across that sandy beach.

So, he hopped and hopped all around;
with the help of friends, he went to town.

Oh, the sights and wonderful smells
of fresh-baked pies on window sills.
The little ant could not resist
the lemon bars and pecan twists.

So, he went inside and filled his tummy
with all things good and yummy!

But when the bill came his way
the little ant could not pay...

So, he washed the pots and pans all day!

It was getting dark and time to go;
the little ant was moving slow.
"Yes!" he cried. "Against a tree,
a shiny scooter, just for me."

But wouldn't you know, it belonged to a boy
who didn't like ants who took his toys.

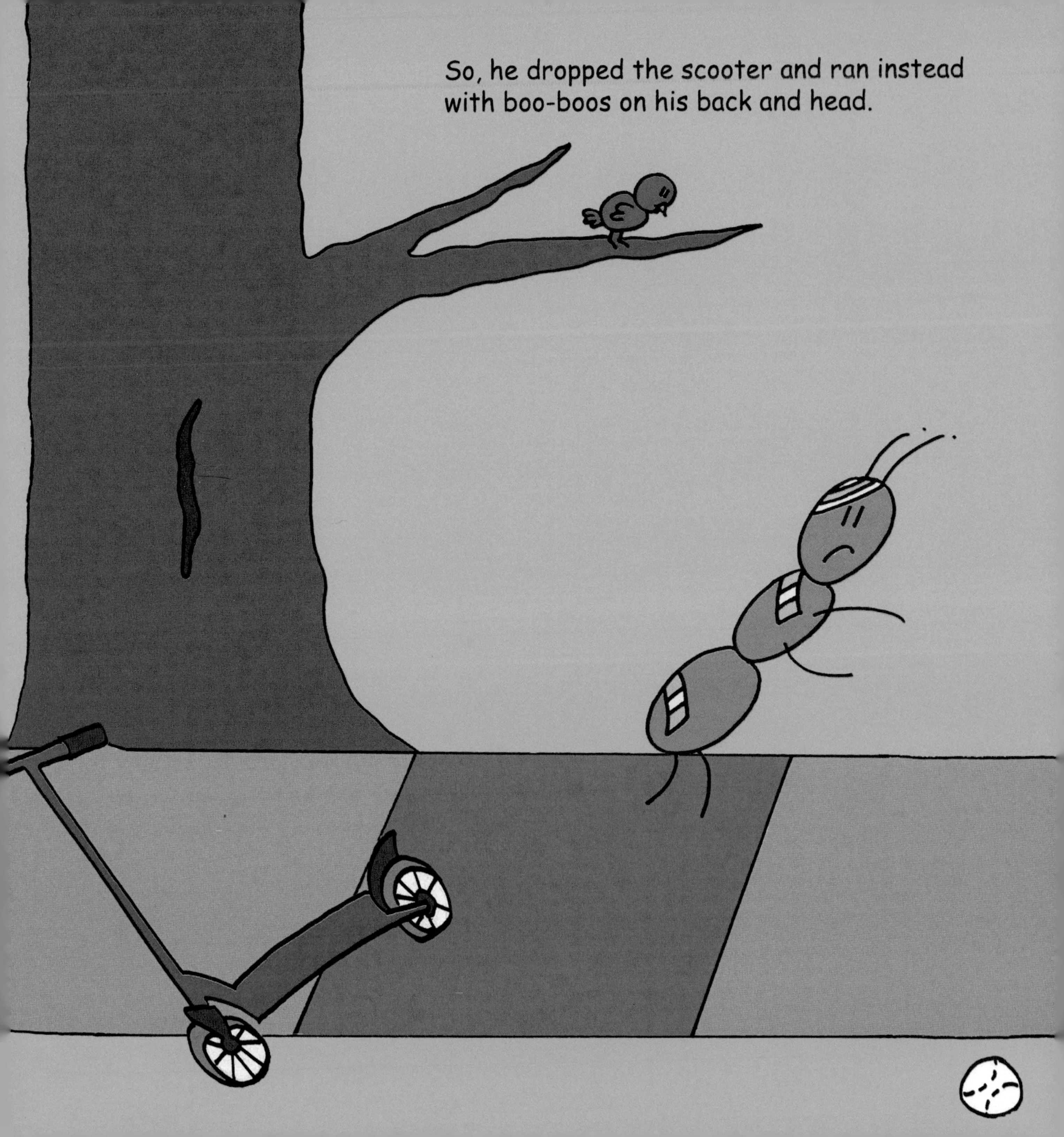

So, he dropped the scooter and ran instead
with boo-boos on his back and head.

Out of breath and out of luck,
his only hope, a passing bus
to get him home without a fuss.

And there it was, for all to see.
"Home sweet home!" he cried with glee.
It was his favorite place to be.

Back to the bathroom, a crack in the wall,
his sweet little mom was starting to call.
She was waiting for him, all in a flurry,
with a whack on the butt for making her worry!

Then a kiss and a hug and a snuggle in bed,
the little ant's journey had come to an end.
Perhaps tomorrow, he would do it again!

The End

Made in the USA
Middletown, DE
30 January 2021

32793256R00015